Dragon Defiant

Dragon Defiant

Lynn Hall

Illustrated by Joseph Cellini

MODERN CURRICULUM PRESS
Cleveland • Toronto

NEW 1984 EDITION

Published by Modern Curriculum Press, Inc.
13900 Prospect Road, Cleveland, Ohio 44136.

Text copyright © 1975 by Lynn Hall.

ISBN # 0-87895-823-1 Paperback
ISBN # 0-87895-797-9 Hardbound

Library of Congress Catalog Card Number: 76-19887

Chapter One

The sky was dark over the back pasture hill, but the hill itself was bright with moonlight on new snow. Near the crest stood a compact white stallion, his red leopard spots blotted out by the crust of snow on his back. He blended so well with his surroundings that only the movements of his mane and tail made him visible.

Dragon pawed at the snow and lowered his muzzle to the grass beneath. He wasn't hungry. There was ample food at the barn, where his mares were huddled in steamy warmth. But he took a bite of the dead grass and snorted, sending a fine spray of snow into the air. This was the first good snow of the year, and he was enjoying it mightily.

He raised his head and looked down at the

lights from the house. Besides the usual yellow squares of light from the windows, there were tiny blue and green lights twinkling in the spruce trees that flanked the front door, and on the roof stood a fat plywood man with one leg inside the chimney.

The decorations were blurred and meaningless to Dragon. The important thing about the house tonight was that Lyle was inside. For the past two years Lyle had been absent from the house except for a few weeks in summer and a few days around the time of the first snow.

While Dragon watched the house, a pair of headlights swung into view and moved slowly toward the barn. They were high headlights, truck size. They swept in a circle from barn to house as the small stock truck backed up to the loading chute beside the barn door.

Dragon tensed.

Truck doors slammed. Lyle's voice, his father's voice, the creaking tailgate, and the sliding sound of the barn door were a familiar medley to Dragon's ears; but he wasn't listening.

He was gathering meanings from the wind. His distended nostrils told him what was coming out of that truck: a stallion.

He flattened his ears and started down the snowy hill at a hard gallop. This was no show-ring confrontation with another stallion, with Lyle on his back and the neutral territory of the arena beneath his hooves. This was a rival stallion entering Dragon's barn, approaching his mares. Age had worn hollows in Dragon's flanks, but his instincts toward his mares and his territory were still in full flare.

He leaped the small stream where Lyle had so often fallen from his back in the early days of their partnership. He thundered along the fencerow beneath the trees where Lyle had first sat on his back. Up the bank and into the barn lot he pounded. The smell of the other stallion was strong. The enemy was inside the barn, where the yellow lights shone and the men's voices rumbled, low and pleased.

The large door leading from the barn lot into the center aisle of the barn was closed and barred with a stout plank. Dragon trotted around the corner of the building. The stallion smell came from behind the window of the first stall, the same stall where Dragon had spent his first terrifying nights on the farm, before it had become his home, his territory.

The window was small and high and full of yellow light from inside. Dragon pushed his muzzle against the cold glass. He couldn't see in because the window was too high; but he could hear, he could smell. There was another stallion in there with Dragon's mares.

Dragon screamed and reared. With a shattering, shimmering noise, the window glass fell away. Now the scent was strong enough to convey the stallion's fear of Dragon and his readiness to fight. The smell of fear and fighting rocked Dragon back to the years in Mexico, the mares that were Dragon's possessions, the stallions who came every year, stallions who needed mares and wanted Dragon's herd. They had to be killed—killed or driven away. It was one of the strongest of the instincts by which Dragon lived. The fact that Dragon was old now, living in the sheltered safety of an Iowa farm, was meaningless when these age-old instincts rose up in him.

Dragon barely heard the shouting, the thumping and banging inside the stall. At first he was unaware of the weight swinging from his head, but eventually it came through to him that Lyle was hanging from his halter. Lyle was a full grown young man now, and his weight began to tire Dragon's neck. With a last angry snort, Dragon dropped to the ground and stood glaring from Lyle to the window with its frame of jagged glass.

"You'd better get that horse back into the truck and away from here," Lyle shouted. "Dragon's going to climb right through that window, and I don't know how long I can hold him."

From inside the barn came Mr. Hunter's voice.

"Why don't you see if you can get Dragon into that stall down at the end of the barn?"

"That won't hold him, Dad. You know he can kick his way out of any of our stalls. Get that stallion away from here. Dragon's going to hurt himself, and I can't hang on to him much longer."

Dragon was rearing again, trying to get through the window despite the drag against his head. There was more shouting back and forth, but doors and tailgates clanged open and shut, the truck door slammed, and with the roar of the truck and the squeak of its tires in the snow, Dragon's enemy disappeared down the lane and away from the farm.

Gradually the pounding and trembling inside Dragon subsided. He stood with his head against Lyle's jacket, weary but satisfied. His territory was safe, and the mares were still his.

Lyle's hand rubbed up his neck, under his mane.

"I told them it wasn't a good idea, old buddy. Dad said you were too old to want to fight another stallion, but he doesn't know you like I do."

Dragon sighed and leaned into the rubbing hand. Lyle was tall and deep-voiced now, and he seldom rode Dragon even when he was home from college; but his hands still knew how to rub.

They were still standing close together, the tall

young man and the aged white stallion, when the truck returned, empty.

Mr. Hunter got out and came into the barn lot. "I took him over to the Johnsons'," he said. "We can leave him there till we get this straightened out, about Dragon. Did he hurt himself?"

The two men led Dragon into the barn and tied him in the center aisle, where the light was brightest. It was warm in the barn. The mares, two dozen of them, milled placidly around the large open area beyond the aisle. They worked at the hay with their long jaws and watched Dragon and the men. Four cats in various shades of yellow came to watch, too.

The light showed several small cuts and a few large ones on Dragon's front legs and chest.

"Nothing too deep," Lyle said. "Where's the gentian violet?"

His father handed him a small brown bottle. "Be sure there aren't any little pieces of glass in those cuts," he said.

"I will." Working carefully, Lyle cleaned each of the wounds and painted them with the purple disinfectant. "Dragon's going to look like a Christmas decoration when I get through with him," he muttered.

"You missed one over here."

When all the cuts had been seen to, Lyle gave Dragon a treat of oats and sank down beside his father on a straw bale. One of the cats came purring up into his lap and shoved her whiskered face against Lyle's chin. The two men stared sadly at Dragon.

"It's not going to work, is it?" Lyle said after a while.

His father sighed. "I really didn't think Dragon would give us any trouble about it—a horse his age."

"Dragon is no ordinary horse, Dad," Lyle said quietly. "He never has been. Any stallion that gets broke at the age of fifteen and then goes on to win an international championship in performance competition isn't going to be ready for retirement at a mere, what is he now, twenty?"

Mr. Hunter began striking his boot with a blade of straw. The cat walked down Lyle's leg and crouched, ready to attack the straw when it came her way.

"I guess you're right, Lyle. But I'm not taking Chieftan back. We need him. You know that. Here we are with a barn full of Dragon's daughters and no one to breed them to. I don't want to breed them back to their own father, and I don't want to be trucking them all over the country and paying high stud fees to breed them to someone else's stal-

14

lions. Buying Chieftan was the only logical answer. He's the ideal mate for Dragon's daughters."

Lyle answered quietly, "And Dragon won't let him on the place."

The minutes passed in silence, while the only obvious answer hung between them.

"You'll be going on to law school after college, anyway, son. And then you'll be settling somewhere, starting your practice. You won't be home enough for it to matter whether Dragon is here or not."

"I know, but . . ."

The barn was still again, except for the soft slapping of straw against boot.

"That corporation up in Michigan made an awfully good offer for him last summer, and I think they'd still be interested. I'll give them a call. He'll have a good home up there, and he should sire some good colts for them before he gets too old. You can see the sense in that, can't you?"

Lyle nodded. "I know you're right, Dad. I just . . . I hate . . . well, old Dragon and I have been through a lot together and I hate to—"

"I know. I know how you feel." Mr. Hunter stood up. "I'm going in the house. You come on in when you've said your goodbyes."

For a long time Lyle sat looking at Dragon. A faraway smile softened his face and his eyes as he remembered.

"You were such a big part of my growing up, Dragon. I wouldn't have missed having you in my life, not for anything. But I guess it's time for moving on now. Time for both of us. Come on, old buddy. You want to go back out to the pasture?"

At the barn door Dragon paused, sensing the sadness in Lyle's voice. But Lyle gave him a strong laugh and a sharp smack on the rump that sent him trotting down the bank and into the pasture.

The cold struck the raw flesh of Dragon's cuts, not with pain, but with the pleasant tingle of wounds from a battle won. He tossed his head and galloped up the hill.

Chapter Two

For the third time in his life, Dragon was traveling north and east toward a new existence.

Eight years before, the first of these journeys had taken him from his home in the Mexican mountains to a life of restricted freedom and uneasy safety on a Texas breeding ranch. That ride had been sheer terror for Dragon, packed into the shifting, roaring, stinking stock truck with the mares who had been his family and his responsibility for as long as he could remember.

The second journey, three years later, had begun more calmly. Dragon had been the only passenger in the Hunters' comfortable horse van, and after his years on the Texas ranch he had become at least somewhat reconciled to people and trucks. But halfway to his Iowa destination, Dragon had felt one of the trailer's floorboards give way under him, and the trip had turned into a nightmare of the fiercest kind of pain.

Later, when Dragon and Lyle had started their show career, horse vans and trailers had gradually become pleasant experiences for the little white stallion. Trips to horse shows had seldom lasted more than a few hours, and usually another horse or two had come along. At the ends of the journeys, the shows themselves had sparkled with challenge and excitement for Dragon. And through all the trips and shows, Lyle had been with him.

On this sunny winter day Dragon rode alone in a small stock truck. He stood knee-deep in fragrant straw and took an occasional pull from the gray green pile of fresh timothy in the hayrack beneath his nose. Through cracks in the truck's slats he saw blue and gold and white slivers of Michigan countryside flashing past.

He felt no fear, just an uneasy knowledge that his life was shifting again, that Lyle had fallen away from him. The past two years had eased Lyle from the center of Dragon's life by gradual stages; so the loss of the boy was by now a gentle kind of sadness.

Fear was little more than a shadowed memory for Dragon. Each year of his life had brought new terrors, terrors that he had met and survived; each experience of survival had added a skin of confidence between Dragon and the world, confidence in his ability to survive. Whether the end result was wisdom or simply the habit of living through threats, Dragon met the world with a steady gaze now. Fear was for the young.

Toward sunset the truck slowed to a stop and backed into an unloading position. When the tailgate opened, Dragon turned to face whoever was coming to untie him. His legs were stiff from the ride, and the outside air smelled good.

"I'll get him." It was a woman's voice, strong and deep. Dragon swung his rear to the side of the truck so that he could more easily turn his head to see her.

The figure that came in beside him could have been either sex and any age. It was clothed in men's green rubber boots, dark khaki coveralls thickly padded against the cold and obviously concealing layers of other wraps underneath, and a hood tied tightly around a broad, flat face. A stray wisp of gray brown hair and a certain softness in her eyes were the only clues that Wilda was female.

She stood beside Dragon's shoulder, stroking him with her square red hand and exploring him with her eyes.

"Dragon," she said. Although her lips didn't smile, all the muscles of her face seemed to lift.

19

"Well, bring him on out," her husband bellowed from outside the truck. "Let's see what we got for our money."

Strong red fingers worked loose the knot in his lead rope, and Dragon followed the woman down the ramp and into a small building not much larger than the truck had been. The shed's original purpose might have been to house chickens, hogs, or sheep, but now it was scrubbed and painted and deeply lined with straw. Hayrack, grain box, water bucket, and salt chunk awaited him. When the woman unsnapped his lead rope, Dragon circled the shed, touching his muzzle to the food and water. Then he swished back to the center of the shed, under the light, and stood waiting for the people to leave.

They stood against the wall and watched him, the woman and the man.

Finally the man spoke. "Well, you wanted him and you got him."

"After all these years of trying to buy him," Wilda said softly. "There he is. Dragon. And he's all ours."

"Part ours," Mr. Ware corrected her. "Ours and the rest of the corporation's. I reckon we'd ought to go in and call them—let them know he got here okay."

The woman didn't answer. Her eyes were on

Dragon, noting the still-purple medicine stains on the cuts on his legs, getting acquainted with the planes of his head, the shape and set of his ears, the arch of his neck that argued with the age-hollows in his flanks and over his eyes.

Mr. Ware spoke again. "I hope I wasn't crazy, letting you talk me into spending that much money for a stud that may be too old to sire colts. They was asking me about it in the barber shop the other day, and I didn't dare tell how much we paid for him; they'd have laughed me out of the shop."

Wilda's eyes stayed on Dragon, but she shook her head, as much as her hood allowed. "He's not too old. You wait and see. Another month or so and the mares will start coming in season, and by this time next year this place is going to be hopping with his colts."

The man rubbed his dripping nose on the back of his work glove and turned to open the door. "I'm going in and call the rest of 'em to let them know he got here. You stand out here in the cold if you want."

She waved a pat in the direction of his arm as it brushed past her, but still her eyes were on Dragon. She began moving around the shed, stirring the straw into place with her boot.

"I'd better be right about you, horse, or that old bird's likely to kick me out of the house, bag and baggage. You are my Christmas present and birthday present for the rest of my life. And Mother's Day."

She came close and rubbed her hand up and down the front of his neck. "Well, I guess there's no sense standing out here all night gloating over you like a kid with a new red wagon. You got everything you need here, and I'll be out again before bed to make sure you're okay." She gave him a dust-raising slap on the chest and left.

When she was gone, Dragon let go of the last bit of tension from the ride. He sank to the straw and rolled.

In spite of the strangeness of the place and its sounds and smells, Dragon slept long and hard through the black time, cocking one hind leg and then the other and hanging his head low. His breath made silvery puffs. The one window at the end of the shed was turning pale when the door opened and Wilda came in pushing a wheelbarrow.

"You're looking fit this morning," she said to him. Working briskly, she pitched his soiled straw into the wheelbarrow, took it away, returned with a half bale of new bedding, and spread it on the bare places. She brought him water and a coffee can of oats. With growing interest Dragon watched her come and go. The oats were fine and the water was welcome, but he hoped for the sight of a saddle and bridle. His mind was alert this morning, his legs were rested from the trip, and a gallop through the icy air was what he needed. But no saddle appeared.

When the woman was gone, Dragon went to the window and touched it with his muzzle. It was full daylight, and he could see the slowly moving forms of horses in a distant field. He whickered softly. No one heard him.

Late that afternoon people came to look at him. They filed into the shed and stood in a line against the wall, talking among themselves. There were half a dozen men and women, all dressed in bulky, warm coveralls and boots and hoods and looking very much like one another; there were a few children, similarly dressed but noisier and more active. One or two at a time the people approached Dragon, ran their hands down his face, along his neck and back, down his legs. The smallest of the children was lifted onto his back while Wilda held his halter. Dragon raised his head, hoping the door would open and Wilda would release him and his tiny rider for a run through the snow. But the child tensed and whimpered and was lifted down, and finally the people left.

When they were gone, Wilda came again and snapped a long rope to his halter.

"Exercise time," she said cheerfully.

Dragon arched his neck and crowded against her in his hurry to get out the door.

"Easy there," she warned. "Until we can get some stallion-proof fencing around the barn lot, you're going to have to get your exercise this way, Dragon. At your age this should be plenty. We didn't have a whole lot of advance warning that you were going to be moving in, old boy, and we've never had a stallion before. Okay, go on."

She stood in the center of the flat area between the barns and the farmhouse yard and played out the rope until Dragon was walking in a wide circle around her. He moved at erratic speeds, walking, dancing, and stopping to stare at the distant horses until Wilda jiggled his halter rope and reminded him to keep going. Under his hooves were ridges of ice and packed snow, and the wind parted his coat and penetrated far up the hollows of his head, but he loved it.

The muscles of his legs were just beginning to stretch into place when Wilda reeled him in.

"That's all for today if I'm going to get supper started. Besides, we don't want to wear you out, do we?"

The next day followed a similar pattern, except that there were no visitors to break the monotony. Wilda did spend some extra time brushing him and checking his hooves in the morning, but the exercise period was again maddeningly short. She came out again after supper and wrapped a measuring tape around his neck just above his shoulders. She muttered a number, then laid the tape out along his side, anchoring it against his breastbone with her hard jabbing thumb and muttering another number. She measured around his barrel again and then left quickly, reciting her list of numbers over and over.

With every day that followed, the small shed became more and more a prison. It was clean, it was comfortably warmed by the heat from his body, there was ample food and water; but there was nowhere to go except around and around in a small circle. Never in his life had Dragon been so confined. Never had he felt so separated from the rhythms of the life around him. People's voices came and went in the distance; cars and trucks and tractors came within Dragon's hearing but left without being seen. The horses in the pasture remained dim, small shapes and slivers of scents that he strained for during his brief moments of false freedom on the exercise rope.

One day the shed was peppered with freezing rain most of the morning. When Wilda came to change his bedding, she said, "No workout on the rope today, old boy. It's slippery as greased glass underfoot, and I'm not taking any chances with you slipping and hurting yourself. Probably tomorrow, okay?"

Dragon spent the evening and most of the night fretting about in his circle. He kicked once or twice at the wall. He stared out the window. In his mind was the feel of his old pasture, his legs driving and pounding along the fence, across the creek, and up the hill, racing with any of the mares that wanted to play or dodging among the trees if the race had to be a solitary one.

By morning Dragon ached with the need to run off the energy that was building up pressure within him. When Wilda opened the shed door, sunlight sparkled behind her.

"Look what I brought you, Dragon."

In her arms was a pile of bright green canvas. She shook it out and spread it over Dragon's back. Buckles fastened at his chest, under his barrel, and beneath his tail.

"There, now. You have a horse blanket as good as any old race horse. Better. It fits just fine." She walked around him, pursing her lips, patting and pulling at the blanket.

Dragon swung his head around and moved his lips over the blanket.

"Oh, no you don't." Wilda pushed his head away. "I worked evenings for a whole week to make that blanket so you wouldn't be cold out here; you're not going to chew holes in it, understand? I've got to get on with my chores, but we'll have a good long workout this afternoon."

The hours passed slowly. Dragon paced in his circle and rubbed against the wall every now and then in an effort to get rid of the blanket. The mild annoyance of the buckles rubbing his neck and the underside of his tail was magnified by the frustration of his confinement.

Eventually Wilda appeared with the long rope. Dragon tossed his head at the exciting sound of the snap against his halter. He made small rearing motions and crowded through the door with Wilda behind him.

"You're feeling your Cheerios today, aren't you, old boy?" She laughed and slapped his rump.

Dragon started his circling at a canter, but he frequently broke his gait to indulge in short fits of bucking.

"Whoa, now," Wilda called. "If you slip on that ice and break a leg, it's me that's going to get shot. Just take it easy."

Dragon slowed to a fast trot, but he arched his neck and jerked against the restraint of the rope with a flip of his head. Suddenly there was a blur of movement and a soft thud. Wilda's bulky form was sprawled on the icy ground.

"Damn," she muttered. The end of the rope lay a foot from her hand.

Dragon stopped trotting and craned his neck to its full length. There was no pull on the end of the rope, no dragging weight. He sidled a few steps, and the end of the rope moved away from Wilda as she crawled toward it.

A sense of freedom spread through Dragon. He danced aside again and snorted. Wilda's voice called to him with a note of panic, igniting his own sudden unsettled feeling. He spun, slipped on the ice, gathered his feet, and trotted in sideways steps away from the woman, who was on her feet now and running toward him.

From Dragon's other side, a dog appeared and began to bark at his heels. The long rope followed him, coming close to his feet, making a slithering noise on the snow.

Dragon saw the lane ahead of him and bolted.

Chapter Three

When Dragon reached the end of the lane, he turned neither right nor left to follow the road, but plunged down into the snow-filled ditch, then did a flat-footed leap across a sagging wire fence. The field that opened before him was rough-plowed and black, most of its snow blown away by the north Michigan winds.

Dragon arched his neck, lifted his tail, and ran. The footing was bumpy, but freedom and excitement lightened his body. Old instincts came back from his mountain days, instincts that set his front hooves down on surfaces that could take them, stride after stride, while his eyes were on the distance.

He leaped another fence. Now the going was easier, over long meadow grass in fragile frozen clumps that broke beneath his feet. He shook his head and lengthened his stride. The long rope slapped a quick rhythm against his neck and rump, reminding Dragon of Lyle's reins and the surging excitement of their barrel-racing days. He could almost hear the crowd noises, almost smell the nervous readiness of the other horses, almost feel the pleasant weight of Lyle on his back. In the barren, frozen meadow, Dragon swerved to the left, then to the right, just for the fun of feeling the balance of his body and the quickness of his legs.

While he ran, the world went from gray blue to deep blue, and gradually the last of the sunset burned itself out. Dragon slowed to a trot. Now and then he stopped to listen to the sounds around him, distant sounds—a barking dog, a truck rumbling along a gravel road, a cow mooing somewhere ahead of him, and always the hissing sound of the wind through the frozen meadow grass. Down lower, there were small rustlings of field mice and rabbits.

Dragon moved on at a fast walk. The rope caught in the brush, and he had to jerk his head to free it. Berry bushes came up around Dragon and gradually merged with woods as the land sloped downhill. Time and again the rope caught. Dragon grew more and more impatient with the delays. By now the rope was feathered with trailing weeds and

small branches. Finally, inevitably, it tangled itself in a stand of sumac and refused to be pulled loose.

Dragon turned to face the maddening rope. He flattened his ears and glared at it. He threw all his weight backward, hard against his halter. It held. He reared, jerking his head to the side as he went up. The sumacs bowed toward him but refused to let him go. He spun and kicked at the bushes but got only a small puncture wound on his inner thigh for the effort.

Dragon's anger mounted. His new freedom throbbed in every muscle of his body; he had no intention of staying tied to a sumac clump.

He sidled over to an oak tree and leaned against it, pressing the side of his head, behind and below his ear, against the bark. With a short, hard movement he pushed his head up and back, dragging the crownpiece of his halter forward against his ears. The halter tightened under his throat; the crownpiece was just over the base of one ear.

He thrust again. The leather choked up hard against his windpipe, but one ear was almost free. One more hard drag against the tree and one ear was out and the other one coming. He tried to turn so that he could rub the other side of his head against the tree, but the rope was too short. He lowered his head and rubbed the halter against the inside of his knee. A buckle pressed painfully against his eyeball.

The halter inched down on his head. Suddenly both ears were free, and the halter was a dead thing falling away to the ground. Dragon reared and came down with his front hooves, grinding the halter into the ground. He snorted with vengeful pleasure, then spun and galloped away.

The land fell away more steeply down the side of the ravine, but Dragon found himself on a narrow path that smelled strongly of cows, so the going was easy enough. At the bottom of the hill lay a stream iced into stillness. The smell of the water beneath the ice reminded Dragon that he was thirsty. He lowered his head to the ice and pawed at it. It refused to break. He pawed harder, but the cold was bitter at the bottom of this sheltered ravine, and the ice was thick. He settled for a few licks of snow.

The path followed the edge of the stream, and Dragon followed the path. The moon was high in the black sky and full enough to illuminate the snow. A fox appeared briefly and watched Dragon pass before it turned and disappeared into the hillside. Dragon shook his neck. More and more often flashes of Mexico came into his mind as the realization of his freedom grew. Not since his capture eight years before had he been in charge of himself; the feeling was like an injection of youth.

The path eventually climbed to flat, open land again, where the wind struck Dragon from the side and followed him. Ahead of him, not far away, some twenty cattle stood near a three-sided shelter. They raised their heads and looked at him. He returned their stares. There was curiosity on both sides, but no threats or challenges. Dragon approached the cattle. As he drew closer, he could smell hay and water and a salt block. He walked among the cows' steamy, warm bodies, through the smell of their manure and their milky udders. They stood their ground and followed him with their eyes as he walked up to the hay bales that lay broken open on the ground.

After the hay, Dragon tried the cows' water. It was in a large, round tank with an electric warmer and it tasted wonderful. He drank long and deep. Ice formed on his muzzle as soon as he came up out of the water, but he hardly noticed it. He found himself a comfortable spot where the wind didn't hit him, and he slept.

The sky was just fading toward gray again when Dragon woke to find his companions walking away from him. They seemed to be following a practiced pattern, spinning down from a round clot of cows to a line of plodding animals moving in single file across the pasture. Dragon watched for a few moments, then fell into line behind them, trotting till he caught up with the last cow. They walked slowly, deliberately. So did he. They turned into a narrow lane between plowed fields. So did he.

The lane turned suddenly around a stand of windbreak pines and opened into a large barnyard. Along the far side of the yard was a mammoth white dairy barn, its doors standing open to swallow the cows, its lights burning warm and yellow in the frigid dawn. Two figures stood in the barn door to usher in the cows, and in the square of light that fell on the ground, a dozen cats converged.

Dragon stopped short. He stared while the cows strolled into the barn, each finding her stanchion. Then, before the men saw him, he turned and trotted swiftly away. It was too soon to put himself back into the hands of people.

He made a wide detour of the farm buildings, then set out to the west. He was in no hurry; he traveled just for the pleasure of traveling, of deciding where to go and then going, without people hanging on his head or shutting doors in his face. He trotted along fencerows, going through open field gates when he found them or over the low wire fences when no gates appeared. When farm buildings got in his way, he circled around them. He crossed roads when he had to, but only when no vehicles were in sight.

As the day progressed, Dragon's bright green blanket twisted farther and farther to the side. The buckle beneath his tail became an unbearable irritant; so he backed up to a stout fence post and sat against it, rubbing until the fabric tore and the buckle fell away. Once the rear anchorage was gone, the blanket slipped farther to the side until it flapped nearly to the ground on his right. Twice his right hind hoof came down on the trailing garment, and twice there was a pleasant ripping sound. After that the blanket was shorter and much less annoying.

As Dragon was crossing a hay field, a rabbit shot up at his feet and streaked away. He snorted and raced after it. When the rabbit swerved and doubled back, Dragon swerved and doubled back. They flew over a straightaway side by side. The rabbit slammed to a stop, veered to the side just behind Dragon, and made a dash for cover. Dragon churned to a stop, too, and followed. It felt as though Lyle should be on his back, adding the balance of his body to Dragon's in the fast turns and cheering him on.

At length the terrified rabbit found his burrow and dived inside, and Dragon slowed to a jog. He moved on in the gradual circle he had been following all day at the guidance of some instinct that knew that one day of freedom would be enough, that by night the little freckled stallion would be ready for Wilda again.

Almost unnoticed at first, horses came into Dragon's senses. The animals' smells and soft sounds were ahead and to the right, beyond a sturdy board fence. Dragon moved faster, head high, ears cocked, nostrils distended. Over the fence he sailed, like a ghost horse in the moonlight. The horses were gathered on the sheltered side of an old hay barn, not quite needing to be inside but enjoying the wind-break of the paintless wooden structure. They lifted their heads as Dragon approached.

He stopped a short distance from them and looked them over. Most were mares: a tall Appaloosa, two neat sorrels who showed Arabian heritage in their heads and high tail sets, one rich mahogany Morgan, and a handful of smaller grade ponies. There were two geldings, a nondescript rusty black and an outsize dapple cream Shetland. Neither of them challenged Dragon's presence.

For a few moments none of the animals moved. Then slowly the Morgan mare came forward. She moved like a queen, bowing slightly with each step, as though she were greeting a visiting monarch whose stature equaled her own. Her muzzle touched Dragon's.

A sense of rightness came over Dragon. This was his place in the world, his function, his work, which he had done so well for so many years. He arched his neck and bit the Morgan on her shoulder.

The other mares began to come up. The Morgan drove them away with peremptory kicks, but Dragon shoved her aside and began a careful inspection of his new herd, except for the geldings, which he ignored. He led the mares on a gallop across the pasture, and they followed him as though it were a habit of years, with the Morgan close behind Dragon and the others a respectful distance from her heels.

As they rounded a clump of young spruce trees, Dragon saw his old shed and the lights of Wilda's house one field away.

It was midmorning the next day when a pickup truck came bouncing into the pasture and stopped beside the barn. Wilda came out one door, her husband out the other, and the farm dog down from the rear. When the mares closed in around the truck, Dragon was in the center of them. The sight and sound of Wilda added the final element to his happiness.

Her voice was tired and strained. "Gather round, girls and boys, and eat up. I've got to get."

Her eyes hit Dragon. She stared. "For the love of . . . Bill! Look here! Look who's here. Oh, my God, what a relief."

Her husband looked up from fiddling with the tailgate. "Hah," he said, pleased. "There's your horse, back again. All by himself. I told you he'd turn up. All that worrying and phone calling and driving around for nothing."

"Dragon." The woman's round, red face was soft with joy. She came through the mares until she stood beside his head. Her fingers touched his neck.

Dragon held his head high. His eyes shone with dignity and peace. There was an understanding between them, the woman and the horse. Their eyes met on a level plane.

From behind them came Bill's voice. "He sure done a job on your new blanket."

"That doesn't matter. He's back, safe and sound. I guess Dragon isn't the blanket kind of horse, anyway."

The man turned and began tossing hay bales down from the pickup. "I think there's a rope in the truck. You want to take him back to the shed?" he called.

She shook her head. "I don't guess this old boy needs all that coddling after all. If he wants to be out here with the other horses, he can stay here."

Bill slammed up the truck's tailgate and climbed into the cab. "Let's get a move on, Mother. We've got work to do."

Suddenly Wilda grinned and moved her face close to Dragon's ear. "Just between you and me, I expect I'd have gone off on a bender, too, if somebody had shut me up like that. You old bugger, I like you." She slapped his chest and left.

Chapter Four

Wilda and Dragon stood in the welcome heat of a steamy May afternoon. She was inside the barn lot's gate, and he was outside, on the pasture side, but his head touched the woman's arm. Every now and then her hand came up to scratch the hollow of his throat.

This was their second spring together, the aging little stallion and the round-faced woman with her wisps of salt-and-pepper hair, her strong voice, and her sure hands. They knew each other's movements and meanings, and they gravitated toward each other as often as possible.

Today they both watched the Morgan mare in the center of the lot and the day-old foal beside her. Dragon had little interest in the colt and stayed at the gate to be close to the woman, but her interest in the foal was absolute.

"There he is, Dragon. He really exists. He's a dream come true."

The foal was a fuzzy rust color with a white blanket-patch over his rump. A neat, narrow blaze divided his face, and both hind legs had white stockings. He stood close to his mother's side and stared around him at the wideness and brightness of this new existence, so different from the warm, wet closeness he could almost remember.

Dragon jerked his head, startled, as a bicycle crashed to the ground beside him. More and more often lately, his ears had failed to alert him to approaching people and animals.

A girl came close to him and hooked her arm over his neck. Wilda shifted to one side and glanced away from the colt long enough to acknowledge the girl's presence.

"I figured you'd show up today," she said.

"I wouldn't miss Dragon's first baby for anything," Abby said. "Is it a boy or a girl? Can I go in and pet him?"

"You better not—not yet awhile, till the mare settles down. He's a horse colt. Just what I wanted. Isn't he something?"

The woman and the girl smiled into each other's eyes in shared appreciation of the miracle. Although Abby promised to become a handsome woman, to a casual observer she was just a collection of uncon-

trolled hair, teeth too large for her face, and a voice so timid it could hardly be heard. But Wilda Ware was no casual observer. To her, Abby was an eager helper with the horses, a quick intelligence, a rare youngster who never rattled on when she had nothing to say that was worth saying.

Abby asked, "Can I sit on Dragon?"

"It's his back," Wilda shrugged. "I don't care who sits on it if he doesn't."

It took three jumps and much leg-kicking to get Abby astride, but Dragon stood quietly. The girl was a pleasant weight on his back, sitting motionless as she always did and scratching his neck under his mane. He was shedding his long winter coat in clumps, and it felt good to be scratched.

The three friends stayed close and quiet, enjoying each other and the sight of the mare and foal in front of them.

"I think Dragon's back is getting bonier than it was," Abby said after a while.

"He's an old horse, Ab. You've got to expect it." Wilda turned and looked up at the girl sitting hunched and motionless on Dragon's back. As so often happened when she watched Abby with a horse, Wilda was rocked, almost physically rocked, back into the young girl Wilda, the twelve-year-old Wilda whose legs ached to wrap themselves around every horse she saw.

Thirty-five years of living and changing and moving and growing had not changed that inner Wilda. They had added size and weight and experiences; they had given her a husband and twenty-three summers and winters here on this farm with a man who was still partly a stranger to her. They had even added horses to her life, those good and disappointing and dull years. The horses had come one by one as concessions that her husband made to her whims. The first horse had come a few years after their marriage from a neighbor whose children had outgrown him. He was a raw-boned, dirty, cream-colored gelding whose bad habits outnumbered his good ones, but he brought Wilda surging relief from a lifetime of horse-longing.

"What are you smiling about?" Abby asked in her quiet little voice.

"Was I? I didn't know. Just looking at you sitting there on Dragon, I got to thinking about my first horse."

"You never told me about him. Were you my age then?"

Wilda shook her head. "I was your age and younger when I first started knowing my life wasn't going to be right till I had a horse of my own, but I didn't get one till I was married. When I was your age, my folks just kept telling me that it was a stage

I was going through and that I'd outgrow it when I got interested in boys."

Abby's face glowed with surprise and pleasure. "That's what mine keep telling me. But you didn't outgrow it, did you?"

Wilda snorted. "Sure doesn't look that way. No, some people do; some don't. You won't outgrow your love for horses."

Abby sparkled. "How can you tell?"

"I can tell. You can take my word."

"You started to tell me about your first horse. What was he like?"

"Oh, yes. Ugly as sin and spoiled rotten. The kids that had him were scared of him—couldn't handle him—so he hadn't been ridden much when I got him. But after we had a few little contests of will, he settled down pretty well. I loved that horse —boy, how I loved that horse."

"Did you have him a long time?"

"About a year was all."

"Why? What happened?"

"Bill sold him. Said we couldn't afford the feed. We were just starting out then, and we didn't have much money. But just between you and me and the fence post. . . ."

"And Dragon."

"And Dragon. Just between us, I think Bill

was jealous. I did spend an awful lot of time off riding when maybe I should have been cleaning house and cooking."

"So then what happened?" Abby propped her arms against Dragon's neck and hooked her feet up on top of his rump.

"I waited a few years till we had a little more money, and then I got another horse. This time I was careful not to slight Bill or the housework, and it worked out okay; then gradually I picked up another one or two along the way. Worked them in on Bill gradually so that he didn't notice that we were in the horse business till we were in the horse business. But they were all just grade horses, cheap ones —never a horse with any breeding behind it."

Wilda's voice softened, and her eyes took on a faraway look. "I've always wanted a good horse—I mean a really *good* animal, with style and quality and breeding behind it. Now I've finally got one." Her gaze focused on the colt.

Abby sat up, offended. "What about Dragon? What about the Morgan mare and your two half-Arabs? They're good horses, aren't they?"

"Well, yes and no. Dragon is a quality animal, as good as I'd ever want, but he has no pedigree behind him, just wild horses. The mares aren't mine."

"Not yours?" Abby's eyes widened. "I thought they were yours."

Wilda shook her head. "I just have them on lease. I could never afford to buy mares that good, especially after all the money we sunk into buying Dragon, and we only own a third of him. So I paid a certain amount of money to the mare's owner for the use of her, for one colt. As soon as the colt is weaned, she goes back to her owner."

Abby thought awhile. "What if she hadn't got pregnant?"

"I'd have been out every cent of money I had, and I'd probably have lost my one chance to get into breeding good horses. And we were taking a real chance, what with Dragon as old as he is. Lots of stallions his age would be past being able to sire colts."

Abby lay down again and wrapped her arms around Dragon's neck. "Dragon is the most wonderful horse in the world. He's going to live forever."

Wilda turned and looked at the girl with a long, sad look.

As time passed, the colt grew and tightened and smoothed out. Even in this spidery stage of his development, he had an elegance that promised to surpass that of his parents. After days of discussion between Wilda and Abby, the colt was christened Justin, after the Morgan side of his ancestry. Abby fought for Dragon II, but Wilda won out.

When Justin was just two weeks old, he and the mare were moved to the pasture, and one of the half-Arab mares took her place in the shed. She emerged with a chocolate-colored filly staggering behind her. One week later the second half-Arab mare produced a tiny white daughter whose skin showed the beginnings of her father's leopard spots. Wilda spent almost all of the daylight hours going from one colt to another, beaming.

On the farms of Dragon's two other co-owners, more of his sons and daughters began to appear. Old Dragon turned out to be worth the money after all, the three families told each other often and with great satisfaction. More mares were already nurturing the seeds of next year's crop of foals, and this year the mares were being shipped in from distant states. When Bill began muttering at the lateness of his supper, Wilda was able to point out smugly that it was Dragon's stud fees that had finished off the car payments and bought new tires for the pickup.

Dragon was unaware of his success. The coming of the colts meant only one thing to him; Wilda spent less and less time talking to him and rubbing his neck. She came to the pasture every day for a good look at all the horses, even the ancient pony gelding, Dickens. She checked the water tank and made sure there were no sore feet or wire cuts on any of the horses, and she gave Dragon her undivided attention for that small bit of time that was allotted to him. But it left him unsatisfied.

When fall came, even Abby's visits dropped off to once or twice a week, usually on Saturday afternoons. From all his years with Lyle, Dragon knew that children tended to disappear at that time of the year and to stay scarce through the winter, but he missed the girl's company.

The old pony, Dickens, began to form an attachment to Dragon and often followed him about the pasture. Since Dickens never moved faster than a walk, it was easy for Dragon to get away from him when Dickens became an annoyance, but more and more often Dragon allowed the fat little creature to stay close to him. Dickens was a poor substitute for human company, but better than nothing.

One day in late October, Dragon became aware of a faint ache in his knees. It had been there a long time, but he was just beginning to acknowledge it. It made him angry and a little frightened, and he galloped around and around the large pasture in defiance of it.

When Wilda came in the pickup that afternoon, Dragon was waiting for her. Today he felt a stronger need than usual for the reassurance of her voice and the sure touch of her hands.

"Hi, Dragon," she said as she stepped down from the truck. "Move over; let me get around.

Here, I brought you some hay. Doesn't look like your grass is going to hold out much longer. Hello, Justin." Her voice ended soft and warm as the colt came trotting up.

As she reached for the colt's halter, Dragon dropped his head between Wilda and Justin and began rubbing his eye against her jacket front.

"Get off, Dragon. You're in my road."

Again she reached for Justin, and again Dragon crowded in between them.

Wilda started to slap him away, but stopped and looked more gently at the long white face that pressed against her.

"What's the matter, old boy? Are you having a bad day? Haven't been getting enough attention lately, huh?" She scratched his chest. "I guess maybe I have been paying more attention to the small fry than to you, but they need me more than you do. They're just babies, Dragon, and you've been taking care of yourself for twenty years. Just because I spend more time with them, that doesn't mean I love you any less—understand?"

She stayed with Dragon until his need was eased; then he moved away from her a little as she turned her attention to Justin and the two fillies. With Dickens close beside him, Dragon watched Wilda drive away. His knees felt a bit better.

Chapter Five

The winter was long and harsh, but it was not an unpleasant time for Dragon. The hay barn in the pasture kept the wind from biting, and the bodies of the other horses were a collection of fragrant furnaces within the building.

Sometime during those months Dickens lost hold of the last of his eyesight. It was a gradual loss and not a vital one. The ancient, dusty dappled pony knew his way around the pasture. Its path and fences and barn and hay pile, its water trough and salt blocks had made up his world for more than ten years, since the last of his riders had grown too tall for him and had sent him to Aunt Wilda and Uncle Bill for his retirement years.

When Dickens could see nothing but a film of gray, his dependence on Dragon's company grew stronger. Often Dragon became impatient with the pony's slow, stiff walk and galloped away from him; but Dragon always circled back after a few minutes and slowed his gait to match Dickens's hobble. When Justin teased the old pony with nips and shoves, nearly toppling him, Dragon intervened, partly from some protective instinct toward Dickens, partly because of the growing antagonism Dragon felt toward the colt, an antagonism that grew as Justin grew.

One morning Dragon emerged from the hay barn and stood with his nostrils flared, reading the air. There was a wetness in it and a green kind of scent. The top inch or so of the mud under his hooves was soft and moist as the frost came up out of the ground. Dragon's breath came more quickly, and he flicked his tail with the first tremors of spring excitement.

Suddenly he turned. The other horses were coming out of the barn, Justin in the lead with the two fillies on either side of him, the big rust gelding, the grade mares, and Dickens last, his eyes unblinking in the morning sun.

But it was only Justin that Dragon saw—Justin, the near-yearling stud colt; Justin, the threat. All of his other springs came into Dragon's mind in a kaleidoscope of fragmented pictures: yearling colts being driven out of the herd, Dragon himself as a cocky yearling being expelled by his sire in a valley in the Mexican mountains. It was spring now. It was time.

With an angry squeal Dragon lunged at Justin. The colt shied away, startled. The other horses scattered.

The movements of the dance were deeply traced in Dragon's mind: the attack, the maneuvers to separate the colt from the other horses and drive him away, the hard bites on neck and sides. Justin was a fine, big, quick youngster, and a smart one, but his defense against Dragon's practiced drive was flimsy. In a matter of minutes, Justin was in the far corner of the pasture with his head lowered in a sulky pretense of grazing. The other horses watched from near the barn, and Dragon stood midway between, holding Justin in his corner with a baleful stare. The pasture fence prevented Dragon from getting rid of Justin completely. That would have to wait for Wilda's help.

When Wilda's pickup finally appeared around midmorning, Dragon was still holding his captive. There was no longer any anger in him toward the colt for daring to exist in Dragon's territory, only pride. His eyes and ears might be losing the fine edge of their sharpness, his legs might be stiffening by infinitesimal degrees; but his mastery of his herd was still intact.

"What's happening here?" Wilda shouted as she plodded through the mud toward Dragon. Her husband followed. Justin started to move toward her, but Dragon cut him off with a swift diagonal drive.

Wilda shouted again, although she was close to Dragon now. "Dragon, you old buzzard, what are you doing to him? If you hurt that colt, I swear. . . ."

"It don't look like the colt's hurt any," Bill called.

Somewhat calmed, Wilda took Dragon's halter in her hard grip. "I'll see if I can hold him," she said over her shoulder, "and you try to get Justin down to the gate and out of here."

Dragon watched calmly while the colt was led in a wide circle around him and out the pasture gate. Then he relaxed, pleased that the job was finished.

Wilda gave him a long, rueful look that was underlaid with fondness.

"I guess I'd better quit underestimating your stallion instincts, hadn't I? It looks to me like we're going to have to do some fencing around here when the ground thaws out, so that you and Justin can have separate pastures. And don't worry; it'll be a few years yet before Justin starts getting the mares."

It was early June, the season when children reappear from their mysterious winter absences, when the Lyle-times had once been all day, every day, rather than small bits of evenings and an occasional sunny Saturday. Dragon leaned his neck into the bite of the wire fence, leaned until the post creaked. His eyes followed the woman and the girl in the next pasture. They were running their hands over Justin and talking across his back while the chocolate and white yearling lipped at their blouses. Dragon nickered, but Wilda and Abby went on petting Justin, not him.

The two had just come from the small paddock where the Morgan mare and the two half-Arabs, leased for another season, were nursing new foals. This year the Morgan had given Wilda a filly—like Justin, dark chocolate with a white rump, but full of feminine elegance. From the Arab mares came a black horse colt and a filly of an indeterminate red. Wilda was vastly pleased with the three of them.

"You've got a little doll of a sister, bud," she said to Justin. "You'd better shape up, here, or she may get to be my favorite."

"Fat chance," Abby said. The words sounded odd in her soft voice.

"Wilda, when are you going to start breaking Justin?" the girl asked as she combed the colt's mane with her fingers. The mane was lying in black finger waves against his neck.

Wilda shook her head. "I'll have to start on

the groundwork this summer, get him bridle-broke and all that. I don't know what I'll do about him next year when it comes time to start riding him."

"Why?"

Wilda snorted. "I'm too big and heavy for him, big old crow like me. He could carry me okay later on, but I don't want him to get too old before he gets manners. And to tell you the truth, I never did get to be what you'd call a whiz, riding. Got started too late, or I just didn't have the coordination, or something. I love my horses with a passion, but I like to enjoy them from the ground. I still want Justin broke, though."

The obvious answer lay shining in Abby's eyes. Wilda looked down into the girl's face, then looked away.

"I know what you're thinking, Abby. I don't know. You're not a very experienced rider." She saw the pain in the girl's eyes, and she knew how important this was to Abby. "It's not your fault. You haven't had much chance to ride, and that's the only way you can learn. I guess I haven't been as much help as I should have been, either. Trouble is, there just isn't much here that you could ride for practice."

"There are lots of horses," Abby offered timidly.

Wilda and the girl looked up together and surveyed the yearlings in this pasture; Dragon, Dickens, and the brown gelding in the main pasture; and the three mares with their infants in the barn lot.

"The mares are out," Wilda said flatly. "They don't belong to me in the first place, and you couldn't get them away from their babies. Dragon, I don't know; I expect he'd be too much for you to handle, even at his age. Dickens is way too old and too little. You'd squash him."

"How about Rusty, then?"

Something in the way Abby said it made Wilda realize that the girl had thought this through before, had been longing to ride the horses, any horses.

"Rusty's not mine, either," she said kindly.

"He's not? I always thought he was."

Wilda shook her head. "Belongs to Bill's niece, Mary Kay. Him and Dickens both. Course, she outgrew the pony years and years ago. She's married now, lives in Lansing. I don't think she has much interest in either of them anymore, but she keeps sending the money for their feed every month, and they stop out maybe once or twice a year, she and her husband. I think she has some idea about keeping them for her own kids if she ever has any, but shoot, Dickens isn't going to last that long. He's close to thirty now. And Rusty wouldn't be what they'd want for kids to start out on, anyhow. Not for you, either."

"How come?"

Wilda shook her head. "Can't trust him, the old buzzard. He never did like being ridden; he used to fight Mary Kay all the way. He was hard to catch in the pasture, he'd fight the bridle, and he'd blow himself up when she tightened the cinch on the saddle. Then, when he wasn't running away with her, he was trying to scrape her off on a fence or a tree or some such. No, I wouldn't put you on him for a minute."

In the silence that followed, Abby fastened her eyes on Dragon leaning against the fence, and Wilda's gaze followed.

"Oh, I don't know," the woman said finally, "old Dragon-horse might not be so bad for you to learn on, after all. He might be kind of quick for you, but at least he's an honest little horse. He'd never try to hurt you. Tell you what, you can give him a try, see how you get along with him. I won't make any promises about you riding Justin next year, but we'll see."

Dragon saw the bridle in Wilda's hand before the woman and Abby were halfway up the pasture lane; eagerly he wheeled and cantered to the gate to meet them. It had been more than two years since a bit had lain atop his tongue, and he had missed the feeling of partnership with Lyle, the boy's body swaying into the turns with his own.

Cautiously Abby said, "I don't know about bareback."

"Best way to learn balance," Wilda stated. "And that old saddle of mine wouldn't fit either one of you. Just take it easy with him till you get the feel of it."

The aging process had sunk Dragon's back just enough to make a comfortable hollow behind his withers, but easy living had padded his ribs. Into this soft depression Abby settled, clamping her knees into the pads of flesh just behind his shoulders. He lifted his head and moved out at a trot.

"Whoa, easy, Dragon."

The bit held him back. The weight of Abby shifted to one side, caught itself as he slowed, and balanced again.

"I'm sorry, Dragon," the soft voice said. "I know I'm not a very good rider yet, not as good as you're used to. But I'm going to learn. I have to learn. Just go easy with me at first, okay?"

They walked along a narrow, deep-worn path through the hillocks of pasture grass, a path trodden by cattle years ago and now followed by the horses simply because it was a path. The grass rolled away on either side, open and inviting and broken only by scattered trees, but Dragon confined himself to the deep rut of the path.

Gradually the stiffness went out of the girl, and

she relaxed into the rhythm of Dragon's nodding head. She sat up a little straighter and let her legs hang more comfortably.

As he felt the changes in his rider, Dragon lengthened his stride until his walk became a running walk, an almost trot, and finally a trot, but a trot so smooth that Abby allowed it and bounced a little off balance only at first.

In the pleasure of the moment, Dragon's mind saw what his eyes did not, the hilly wooded Iowa pasture. He felt the teetering of the unsteady boy on his back; he heard Lyle say, "Whoa, easy, Dragon."

His legs burned with the need to run. The excitement of having company with him, up behind his ears, talking to him and going where he went, was urging him on. He had to answer the pull at his mouth with a counter-pull against the bit.

The hill in the Hunters' pasture loomed in front of his eyes, overlaying the Michigan flatland. The creek was there coming at him, the creek that had mysteriously taken Lyle from his back in their early rides.

Dragon broke into a canter and leaped the stream.

A small squeal woke him to the present. His back was empty. He slammed to a stop and turned.

Abby was rising stiffly on one knee, looking at

a green-stained elbow, getting up swiftly and coming to Dragon.

He lowered his head into the circle of her arms. "Did I hurt your mouth? I hope not. I tried not to pull on the reins when I fell. Are you okay?"

Dragon's placid gaze reassured her.

"Well, then what made you jump like that?" she demanded. "There wasn't a thing in the world to jump over—nothing but plain old cow path. Otherwise, I'd have been hanging on better."

She flung herself across his back and kicked her legs until she was up.

"I had my first fall," she said with a note that was close to pride in her voice. "It wasn't as scary as I thought. Heck, you can't hurt me."

Her legs pressed him into a trot, and they crossed the broad pasture with their heads up and their hearts full of summer.

Abby came every day that summer, and every day Dragon was waiting for her. They rode in the pasture with Dickens struggling to keep up. They rode the two miles into town later on, when Abby's confidence was equal to it. Dragon carried her along sidewalks and among barking dogs, between cars and in front of trucks with a steadiness that completely masked his early years as an untouched stallion and his middle years, filled with terror and punctuated by the pain of a truck crashing out of the night at him, slaughtering his mares, and cracking Dragon himself.

September came, and the Labor Day parade, and Dragon carried Abby at a slow prance just behind the high-school marching band. Abby grinned until her face ached.

After that their rides were fewer and shorter, but by then the job was mostly done. Abby's natural ability was borne to the surface by Dragon's combined high spirits and kindness; by winter she was, if not yet expert, both competent and confident.

Chapter Six

The bitter Michigan winter brought the end of the riding and the return of the stiffness in Dragon's legs. This time the stiffness was more painful, more persistent. He galloped longer and harder around the frozen pasture, pounding the stone-hard ground in his anger against his legs and making them worse.

Dickens slowed down noticeably that winter. He never trotted anymore but walked more and more slowly, listening for Dragon with ears almost as useless as his eyes. Sometimes Dragon stood close to the ancient pony and stared down at him as though he were trying to understand what was happening to Dickens.

But if summers were passing more and more quickly for Dragon, winters were, too, and again the pasture began to soften into gentler days. On one warm afternoon the ground turned from mostly white to mostly tan with an under-tinge of green.

Dragon was watching over the fence on the April morning when Abby started up the lane with the bridle in her hand. He raised his head and forgot his aching knees.

But she stopped short. She opened Justin's gate instead. "I'll be over to see you pretty soon," she called to Dragon. But it was Justin she rode that day.

That spring there were fewer mares to be bred, but every mare that had been brought to Dragon the year before gave birth, and every colt had the look of Dragon about him.

It was a time of dual emotions for Dragon. On a hot, still, blue-sky day he might stand under the same tree for hours, swishing flies from his own back and Dickens's. He would watch Wilda and Abby and Justin working in the distance and have no desire to be anywhere else, doing anything else. At these times his mind often saw flashes of Mexico or Texas or Iowa, but the pieces of his life fitted comfortably with each other, and with the last piece of it, this time and this place.

On other days, especially when the air was thick and heavy with the coming of a summer storm, Dragon trotted restlessly from one fence to the other. He felt anger at his legs, ears, nostrils, and all the parts of him that worked more slowly or more painfully or more dimly than they should. He felt a sense of something in the future for which he was not ready. At these times he disliked Dickens and avoided him.

The weeks and months passed in a cycle that seemed faster and faster to Dragon. He had barely adjusted to summer when the leaves on the pasture trees changed color, fell to the ground, and were covered by the snow of another winter.

On a day in February Dragon heard Wilda's voice and the sound of hammering. He followed the sounds to the pasture gate, near the small barn lot and shed. Wilda, wrapped to the tip of her red nose, was nailing two-by-fours to the fence posts and stout planks to the two-by-fours. Bill was helping. In their thick overalls, the two figures were identical except for Wilda's voice, her wisps of gray hair, and a corner of a plaid scarf that stuck out from her drawstring hood.

When she saw Dragon, she straightened from her pounding and took a moment to rub her mittens against his neck.

"Hi, old boy. We're getting your fence all fixed up for you here."

"I still think you're crazy," Bill muttered.

Wilda returned to her work. "Take the other

end of this board. No, higher. That's it. I don't care what you think. Dragon is not going to the kill market."

Her husband shook his head as much as his clothing allowed, which wasn't much. "You got your good young stallion now, and you got some good two-year-olds and yearlings coming up. I think you're throwing away feed, keeping that old horse. I don't care how famous he was when he was younger; he's got sons and grandsons all over the Midwest that are better than him. Nobody's going to be paying us stud fees to breed to Dragon anymore."

Wilda didn't answer.

Bill went on. "And then standing out here when it's twelve below zero, fixing fence for a worthless old horse that ought to go to the—"

"You don't have to help," Wilda snapped. "I didn't ask you to help, but I'll tell you one thing, mister: Dragon is *my* horse; he's the first good horse I ever had in all my years of wanting one and having to wait because you had to have a new manure spreader or a new part for your tractor or some such. And that horse has given me more than I could ever give him if he lived another thirty years. And by God, he's going to live out his life here in comfort AND in safety. If that means building this fence up higher so he and Justin can't get at each other when the mares start coming in season, then that's what I'm going to do, twelve below zero or not."

She whammed the nail so hard she split the board.

Dragon awoke by gradual stages. He had spent the night outdoors in the mud circle of his small barnyard, as he had every night since he and Dickens had been moved in from the pasture. Before he opened his eyes, his other senses were registering the warmth of the air, the wet smells about him, and the good feel of the mud packed into his hooves.

His eyes opened. He turned and looked into the open shed behind him. Dickens lay curled like a dog in the deep straw. With sucking noises at every step, Dragon went to the pony and touched him with his muzzle. Dickens twitched, moved one leg, cracked open one filmed eye. Dragon snorted and moved away from him. When he slept and right after he woke, there was an essence of stillness about Dickens now that disturbed Dragon—a slowed rhythm to his breathing; a different, harder feel to his skin.

Dragon moved back out into the sun. He sorely missed the freedom of the pasture, but the barn lot did offer one consolation—the sounds from the house. Today he could hear music from the kitchen radio,

Wilda's voice shouting to Bill, and small clattering kitchen sounds of metal and glass.

The new boards around the top of the fence were so high that he had to stretch his neck a bit to get his head over the top, but he made the effort this morning and laid his long jawbone atop the fence. He could see the house, but it was more blurred than it used to be.

When Wilda came out the back door, Dragon whickered softly, eager for company, but she didn't hear him. He shifted his head and watched as she walked toward the far pasture. In a few minutes she came back leading Cinnamon, the leopard-spotted white filly who was the product of Dragon's first breeding with the half-Arab mare. Cinnamon was a light and lovely three-year-old now, a feminine counterpart of Dragon himself.

Suddenly Dragon tensed. The mare was ready to breed. His ears stiffened. His neck arched as it had for twenty years in response to mares in spring.

But Wilda and Cinnamon walked past him and through the gate into Justin's territory. Dragon watched, enraged, while Wilda tied the mare to the fence and led Justin to her.

A lifetime of instincts burned through Dragon. He flattened his ears and squealed. He spun, half-reared, and galloped in a tight circle, then straightened and rushed the fence.

He gathered himself and leaped. The top board struck the underside of his ribs, scraped his belly, cracked his stifles, then broke as Dragon came down hard, but with his feet under him. He felt nothing except the urgency of the mare and Justin.

Across the lane he pounded; then he flew over the low pasture gate. He squealed. Justin spun away from the mare, startled. Wilda yelled something.

There was joy in the pounding of his blood. The Mexican mountains swam into the backdrop of his view as he focused on this strange marauding stallion that had come to steal Dragon's mares.

He screamed and lunged. His teeth caught Justin in the throat, but, oddly, his jaws refused to lock in their killing grip. Justin slipped away.

A hoof raked open Dragon's shoulder. A red stallion head snaked in under his vision, and suddenly there was a frightening cutting pressure blocking off Dragon's breath.

Somewhere a bird or a woman screamed.

Dragon twisted free and struck again. Years of disuse had somewhat dulled his fighting instincts, but Justin had never fought. Age and inexperience balanced each other.

With thuds and grunts the two sweating bodies collided again and again until Dragon was caught off balance. He went down but scrambled away

before Justin's hooves came driving down. Before his conscious mind knew he had fallen, he was up again.

Every nerve and muscle within his hide gave more than it had. He reared and drove into Justin with hooves and teeth.

But Justin danced away.

Suddenly the earth tipped and spilled Dragon through sky and grass; Justin was above him, eyes wide, nostrils flaring, hooves coming down, down.

But it wasn't Justin above his head, and it wasn't hooves coming down. It was Wilda's face and her fist holding a dripping rag. Dragon could see the familiar face only dimly, but he smelled the salt of her tears.

Gradually his awareness spread. One of his eyes was pressed against Wilda's lap. The shed was around him, and pain was around him and through him in every part of his body. He could almost feel pain in the ends of the long hairs of his tail. His belly felt as though someone had peeled off the skin, his hind legs ached unbearably, and his throat was so swollen that every breath was a battle.

There was a stir behind his head, and Abby's face appeared.

"Oh, no!" the girl whispered. "What happened?

I saw the vet's truck go by, and I got here as fast as I could on my bike."

Wilda shook her head. "They had a fight, Dragon and Justin. I was just getting ready to breed Justin to Cinnamon."

"But how did Dragon get out?"

"Over the fence. Through it as much as over it," Wilda said shortly.

"Oh! What about Justin?"

"He's okay. Hardly even bled." There was a note of something near bitterness in her voice.

The girl heard it and understood. She dropped to the straw beside Wilda and laid her hand against the bones and veins of Dragon's face.

"Dragon lost his last fight," she said softly. "But think of all the fights he must have won, back when he was a wild stallion. He must have won all of them, Wilda, or he wouldn't be alive today. And what other twenty-three-year-old horse could have gotten over that fence and would have had the guts to start a fight like that in the first place?"

Wilda said nothing, but she wrapped her arm around the girl's shoulder for a sharing of comfort and support.

Abby said, "Look at poor Dickens; he looks so scared."

The pony stood trembling in a corner of the shed, straining his useless eyes and nearly useless ears, trying to know what was happening beside him in the shed. Dragon was there, but lower down than he should be, and blood and medicine and fear-sweat were in the air.

Wilda and Abby stared for a long, soft moment at the old dappled pony. When Wilda spoke, her voice came out low and hard. "I pray to goodness that Dragon doesn't get like that, that old, that helpless."

"Is Dragon very bad now? What did the vet say?"

Wilda spoke more briskly. "He's bad, but he ought to make it through this. Doc thought he might have cracked one or both of his stifle joints on the fence. Tore up his underside pretty badly—see where he stitched him up? And I have to keep ice packs on his neck to keep the swelling down, so that he doesn't choke to death. Other than that, just cuts and bruises and maybe some cracked ribs."

"I can help," Abby said. "If this had to happen, it's good it was on a weekend. We can take turns. It must have been awful, the fight."

Wilda shuddered. "It was hell. Bill wasn't here, and I couldn't get hold of Justin's rope. It kept swinging around in the air, but I couldn't get it. I guess I was yelling; a couple of men going by in a truck stopped and came running in. They grabbed hold of Justin's rope just about the time poor old

Dragon was going down for the last count. They hauled Justin off him and got him quieted down, and then we got Dragon to his feet and got him in here—how, I'll never know, but we did. And then one of them called for the vet, and then they left. I don't know who they were; I can't even remember if I thanked them or not."

After a long, quiet time Abby said, "I wonder what your husband's going to say."

"He's going to say I told you so. And he did. He told me I was asking for trouble, keeping two stallions on the place. But I never had any idea Dragon could get over that fence, the way we built it up. Now I'm going to have to fight Bill again about sending Dragon to the kill market."

The girl was silent.

"All I want," Wilda said slowly, "is for Dragon to live out whatever life he has left in comfort and with some kind of dignity. I don't want him to end up like poor old Dickens. But damn it, Dragon isn't ready for a bullet between the eyes, either. Not yet awhile."

Chapter Seven

Around midnight, Dragon pulled his legs under him and struggled to his feet. Standing, he felt somewhat better.

Outside, the night had turned chilly, but there was a pastoral coziness inside the tiny shed. The one yellow light bulb shone through its dust and cobwebs to give an illusion of warmth with its light. Dickens had long since relaxed and was curled in one corner in his doglike resting position. On the stairsteps of straw bales in the opposite corner, Wilda and Abby sprawled. The girl's legs and feet were wrapped in one of Wilda's old quilts. A bale beside them held empty pop bottles, a coffee thermos, and a litter of potato chip bags and dishes from the house. A tiny portable radio hung from a nail above their heads, but the last of the local stations had deserted them at midnight, and the shed had grown still.

The two brightened as they watched Dragon come to his feet.

"He's going to be okay," Abby said.

They had taken turns saying, "He's going to be okay," all afternoon and evening, but this time there was certainty in the girl's voice.

"I should shoo you off home," Wilda said. But neither made a move.

"I'll stay awhile."

With the immediate concern for Dragon receding, Wilda and Abby expanded in a shared quiet enjoyment of the moment, of being in this dusty yellow square of space in the center of a black world, with Bill asleep at the house, everyone asleep but them and Dragon. For Abby it was a precious chance for a long, uninterrupted time with the person she valued above anyone else. It was an important instant in her life, she knew without knowing why.

For Wilda, this night was the top of many translucent layers of memories of other midnights in other barns. She smiled.

Abby sat one bale above and behind Wilda on the loose stairstep pile, but she saw the smile in the curve of Wilda's already round cheek.

"What are you smiling about?" Abby was nearly grown now, longer and thinner than before, but still quiet-voiced and unsure of herself with any but horses and Wilda.

"Just remembering." Wilda's smile broadened. "I was remembering the first time I spent the night in a barn."

"Tell me. If it isn't private."

Wilda laughed. "No, not private. I was about eight or nine years old, I guess. I ran away from home, and I was going to hire myself out to this place. It was a kind of run-down old riding stable outside of town, and it was where I had decided I wanted to live. I figured they could either hire me or adopt me, one or the other. I remember I hid in the ditch till after dark, and then I got into the stable and hid in an empty stall, but the dog made such a racket that I was more scared than anything else. The man came out, found me, and took me home—that was that."

For a long moment Abby grinned at the back of Wilda's head; then she said, "I have to confess. I always wanted to run away and come here, when I was little."

"Because of the horses?"

"Yes."

"And now, here we are."

After a minute Abby said, "It makes me feel good, that you used to want horses as much as I do now, and that you finally got them."

Wilda snorted softly. "They can say what they want to about the joys of youth, but believe me, it's better when you get control of your life. If you handle it right, that is."

"Like how?"

"Oh, knowing what you want and going after it in a practical way. I wanted horses, so I married a farmer."

Abby chuckled. "That makes sense, I guess. But why didn't you marry someone who loved horses as much as you did?"

"I don't know for sure. Instinct, I guess. I didn't think it through at that age, but looking back, I guess I wanted to be the horse person of the family. I wanted to be in charge, not just the wife of somebody who had horses. When Bill came along, I must have sensed that I could handle him, that he'd let me have my horses and wouldn't interfere. And he was already farming with his dad when I met him."

Abby said hesitantly, "It sounds kind of . . ."

"Calculating?"

"Well—"

"It's just sensible, and don't you forget it when your turn comes, my girl. When you pick out a husband, you're picking out the way you're going to live. If you get one that's richer or poorer than how you want to live, or a man that can't be happy living in the country while you can't be happy living in town, then you've got nobody but yourself to blame when you find yourself stuck somewhere you don't want to be, and no happy way out of it."

"Could I ask you something personal?" Abby said softly.

"You can ask. I may not answer."

"Do you feel—I don't know how to say this— do you feel like you're an entirely different person from when you were my age, or do you feel just the same only older, or what? I try to picture myself being twenty and thirty and forty and fifty, but I just can't imagine it."

Wilda nodded. "I know what you mean. Here I am forty-three, and I can't imagine myself sixty or eighty. And when I was sixteen, I could no more picture myself forty-three than the man in the moon." She thought awhile. "I feel pretty much the same. There aren't as many mysteries now, of course. I know what I'm going to look like when I grow up" —they both laughed—"and I've been through things, losing my parents, almost losing the farm a time or two. Came near losing Bill once when his jacket caught in the corn picker, so I know how I react to bad times. That's good to know."

"Do you think you changed, then, as you got older?"

"No, not changed. I got more *myself* as I got older is all."

Abby frowned. "How do you mean?"

"Well, just that I got firmer. When I was your age, I was sometimes nice to people and occasionally not so nice, and sometimes honest, and other times I lied. And then I'd go back and forth between being scared of people and being too talky and too pushy. Things like that. The horses were about the only constant thing about me. Then, I guess, as I got older, the things that were really my nature got stronger, and the rest dropped away."

Dragon took a step toward them and hung his head where the two could rub him.

"He's walking," Wilda said. "Those stifle joints can't be banged up too bad, can they?"

"Good old Dragon. You're going to make it. How old is he, anyway, Wilda?"

The woman shrugged. "Probably around twenty-four; it's hard telling. Around there, though."

The shed was quiet.

In a near whisper Abby said, "Are you afraid— about dying, Wilda?"

Wilda looked sharply across Dragon's face at the girl.

"Are you? At your age?"

Abby shook her head. "Not really. I know in my head that everyone dies and that I'm going to, someday; but at the same time I just don't believe it.

I just can't believe it's ever going to happen to me."

"Everybody feels that way, I guess. I think about it sometimes. I did when my parents died, although I was thinking more about their lives than about death. I wondered if they'd gotten everything they wanted out of their lives. I never really knew them very well, and that made me sad at the end."

"How about you, though? Does it bother you a lot, knowing that you've used up probably half of your life already? And that you're going to have to face it someday?"

Wilda looked up at the shed roof for a long time. "I don't mind it as much now that things are finally getting started for me. I'm a horse breeder, and I've got good stock, thanks to Dragon; so I'm finally beginning to feel as though I, or my horses, rather, will leave something good behind me on this earth after I'm gone. If I let myself think about it, I'd bitterly resent that I didn't get an earlier start at it, so that I could be into my tenth generation of horses of my own breeding instead of just starting the second generation. But other than that, I'm pretty content.

"I'd like to live another thirty-five or forty years, as long as I'm healthy and active, and then die before I get to the point where I'm helpless and a burden to other people. I expect that's what everyone wants. If I were to find out tomorrow that I was about to die, I'd hate it like fury; but I think most old people are ready to go when the time comes."

Abby shuddered. "I can't imagine ever being ready to die."

Wilda gave the girl's foot a squeeze. "Nature does a pretty good job of getting people ready for it," she said warmly, "unless they're cut off before their time, in an accident or something."

"You mean the way older people gradually lose their—what would you call it—keenness? The way they slow down and get forgetful, and don't see and hear so well anymore? My great-grandmother can't ever remember us kids' names or which generation we are. She keeps thinking my brother is my father, and she calls me Betty all the time. The little kids make fun of her, but she always seems so sort of, I don't know, soft and sweet and vulnerable. She's kind of like a child herself."

"That's it exactly," Wilda said. "Nature seems to take people in a kind of a circle; as though the closer their bodies get to death, the closer their minds get to the beginning of their life. I don't really understand what death is, except that it's a necessary part of life."

Abby pulled Dragon's head against her chest. "I wish the horses didn't have to die, though."

"The old ones have to make room for the new ones. You and I love Dragon, but we love Justin, too, and the young colts. Eventually they'll all die to make room for the next generation, and every generation should be better than the last, if the horses are bred right."

"I know, but—"

"Dragon's father had to die to make room for him," Wilda said gently. "Maybe not that one specific horse dying to make room for that one specific colt, but you know what I mean."

They were quiet for a long time. Then Abby said softly, "But I'll miss him when he's not here any more."

And Wilda answered, "So will I, Abby. Not all the Justins in the world will fit exactly into the hole Dragon will leave."

The two voices made a pleasant overlay in Dragon's mind as he stood on his aching legs, but there was a stillness inside him that had never been there before.

Chapter Eight

That summer, when the breeding season was safely past, Dragon and Dickens were returned to the back pasture.

"He needs green grass and trees around him," Wilda said to Abby as they escorted Dragon down the lane. Dragon moved almost as slowly as the pony who followed at his flanks. His battered stifle joints had healed, but they were stiff and painful.

Throughout the long summer the two elderly animals stood head to tail under the trees, their eyes half-closed to the swift movements of the half-dozen yearling fillies who shared the pasture. The days blurred into one another in Dragon's mind. He slept and woke with no clear awareness of night and day.

When he closed his eyes, he saw with great

clarity the brilliant sunlight glimmering across the purple gray water of a mountain lake. He leaped and rolled and splashed in the water, then bounded out, flapping himself like a wet puppy. His mother was there, but she kicked him away when he tried to nurse.

Sometimes he saw a huge old white stallion standing over him, nosing over him as Dragon lay near his mother's legs—or was it the ancient dappled pony who lay curled in the straw? Dragon flattened his ears and attacked the white stallion—because he had to, because it was time for the mares to belong to Dragon. But somewhere a woman shouted, "Justin! Dragon!" and the old white stallion moved slowly away into the mountains, carrying the ache of defeat.

Dragon awoke from one such sleep to find Wilda and Abby coming into his vision. Now things were closer to him before he saw them. His eyes registered only faintly the grass around him, brown instead of green, and the leaves of the trees, underfoot instead of overhead. Wilda wore her winter coveralls and her old plaid scarf, and Abby looked childishly round again in her layers of jackets and sweaters.

"Are you going to bring them in?" Abby asked. Dragon moved toward her and pressed his head against her jacket front in their accustomed greeting.

"I don't know," Wilda said, sighing. "I probably should; it's supposed to get colder tonight. But I hate to. Dragon seems so much happier out here than in the shed. Let's give them another day or two of freedom—it's going to be a long winter."

Abby cocked her head and studied Dragon as she rubbed his chest. "He hasn't snapped out of it, has he?"

"Who, Dragon? You mean from the fight with Justin?" The four of them, two women and two old ponies, turned and walked slowly toward the pickup truck just inside the pasture gate. Wilda let down the tailgate and, with Abby's help, began tossing hay bales out onto the ground.

"No, I think you're right, Ab. He has seemed sort of, well, defeated since then. He's probably got some aches and pains he didn't have before, but I think it took something out of his spirit, too."

"I don't know, though," Abby said thoughtfully. "He doesn't seem unhappy, just kind of resigned; as though he understands that the useful part of his life is over. I wonder if horses can understand anything about getting old and dying, or do they just wonder why their bodies don't work as well as they used to?"

"I have no idea. Here, grab the other end, will you? There we go. I don't suppose they have the fear of dying that people do; they couldn't very well. They couldn't have any way of knowing about it.

That in itself would be a blessing. I know people who let their whole lives be shadowed by their fear of death. Seems a shame, I've always thought."

The figures jumped down, the tailgate clanked shut, and the pickup rolled through the gate. Abby, standing beside the gate to close it, turned and waved to Dragon.

"See you tomorrow."

Dragon watched till they were out of sight, then lowered his head to the hay and began to eat. Suddenly he looked up at Dickens. The pony wasn't eating. The fillies were working on another bale a little distance from Dragon and Dickens, so there were no crowding bodies keeping Dickens from the hay. Dragon walked over to him and touched him on the shoulder with his muzzle. There was a disquieting stiff unsteadiness in the pony's stance.

Dragon walked around Dickens and nudged him gently in the direction of the hay. Dickens took one short step to steady himself, but that was all. For several minutes Dragon stood beside him, watching, waiting for Dickens to follow him back to the hay. But when Dickens continued to hold his braced stance, Dragon left him and finished off the hay himself.

Twilight turned to night, and Dragon moved toward the barn with the fillies.

Dickens remained fixed to his spot, but when

Dragon was far away from him, the pony whinnied. Dragon went back and stood beside him.

The moon came up, and the wind rose. To Dragon, it smelled of snow in the distance. The two-inch-long dusty dappled fuzz on Dickens's hips stood straight up in the wind.

Dragon lifted his head and fixed his eyes on the pony. Something was happening. Dickens's sightless eyes opened wide and seemed to focus on something in front of him. He threw back his head and shied. Stumbling, clattering, half-falling up the hillside, the pony bolted.

Dragon followed.

He couldn't see, hear, or smell whatever it was that Dickens fled from; yet, in a part of his mind that saw without the help of his eyes, Dragon had a sense of narrowing darkness with a spreading light beyond it.

Dickens cantered as fast as his stiff old legs could make the motions. A tree appeared in his line of flight, and he crashed into it. But by the time Dragon had caught up to him, Dickens was on his feet again and moving. His speed was slower because one foreleg dragged uselessly from a cracked shoulder, but his fear was more intense.

He veered off at an angle and fell again, brought down by the uneven footing.

He stood. He was rigid. His head was higher

than it had been for years. His nostrils flared and his chest heaved.

The narrowing darkness grew more intense. Dragon shook his head and stood at a short distance from Dickens, his own heart pounding in rhythm with the pony's.

For an instant Dickens fixed his filmy eyes on Dragon, and the tension drained away. The fear was gone. The pain was behind him, and the narrowing dark became spreading light. Dragon felt the light, felt it shimmering around Dickens, and felt the relief.

The pony sank to the ground.

For a long time Dragon stood over the empty pile of hair and bones. Over and over he saw the fear in Dickens's eyes and the helplessness of his last flight.

Dragon moved away. He tossed his head and quickened to a trot. He did not stumble against trees or fall over clods of frozen mud. His eyes saw obstacles and his feet avoided them, as they had for all the years of his life. When he asked his legs to extend in a gallop, they did.

Something was beside him, not Dickens now, but a small white filly flecked with her father's red freckle marks. She was a yearling and could run with the speed of an adult horse, but Dragon maintained his lead.

His heart felt lighter.

The pasture gate was ahead of him. He leaped and the filly followed. Away from the house he turned, away from Wilda, whom he loved but had no further need of. They crossed a hay field, gaining speed. A few snowflakes blew into Dragon's face as he ran, but then they became a spray of sand from the floor of the mountain valley where the mares went to foal each spring.

Down a ravine they plunged, across a frozen stream, and up the other side. Here there were no fences, just frozen Michigan plains billowing with iced humps of prairie grass.

The two colts raced across the valley floor, wild with freedom. Behind them grazed the mares who gave them life and the old white stallion who protected them and kicked them away if they crowded him. The sun was strangely cold, and the sand came faster and faster against his face, but the young Dragon opened himself to the fight against wind and gravity.

Across the snow-frosted prairie came a light and a roaring sound as the Great Northern diesel clattered through the night, pulling a hundred and twenty cars of passengers and grain from Montreal to Duluth.

Dragon saw it and heard it and felt it—felt the rumbling of a thousand hooves and the scream of the challenging stallion. He veered and raced beside the tracks.

The men, the cowboys with their swinging ropes, were behind him, driving his starving mares into a canyon from which there was no escape, no escape but the running. Dragon extended his neck and flattened his body to the ground. He knifed through the wind and the driving snow and gloried in them.

The filly dropped back, and Dragon was racing alone, Dragon and the mammoth diesel engine beside him.

Dragon sensed a looseness and a strength in his legs that were not limited by the years. No stiffness held him back now.

At the outside edges of his eyes he saw the beginning of the narrowing darkness. It was right. It was welcome.

It was time.

For Dragon there was no blind stumbling terror, no falling and rising and piteous dodging. His challenging neigh echoed down the black tunnel, and his legs pounded faster, harder, stronger—toward the light at the end.

About Dragon

No one knows for certain the origin of the Mexican mustangs, small horses that live in the Sierra Madre in Michoacán, Mexico. But the generally accepted belief is that they originated from a handful of Spanish Barb horses that were being brought to Mexico to aid in the Spanish Conquest in the sixteenth century.

The changes were great, from the large, highly bred, solid-colored Barbs to the small, sturdy, spotted mustangs, and yet one quality, more important than size or color, binds them together. It is the quality of adaptability, coupled with an unconquerable will to live. And it is this quality that the small but rugged Mexican mustang called Dragon had in great quantity.

Born in the Mexican mountains more than twenty years ago, Dragon was captured at about the age of twelve, brought to Texas, and registered with the Pony of the Americas Club as Dragon No. 103. For three years he lived on a ranch near Dallas and sired the scores of outstanding POA ponies who were to bring him fame. These offspring bore not only Dragon's Appaloosa markings but also his courage, stamina, intelligence, and spirit. Through them, Dragon became recognized as one of the foundation sires of the POA breed.

At around fifteen, an age when most horses are considered old, the little white freckled stallion began a new career that called for all the swiftness and sharpness of instinct that kept him alive in the wild. Under the loving hand of a young Iowa boy, he was broken to ride and learned the demanding art of Western performance competition. He was named an International Performance Champion in 1961 at the Third Annual International Pony of the Americas Show.

ABOUT THE AUTHOR

Lynn Hall was born in a suburb of Chicago and was raised in Des Moines, Iowa. She has always loved dogs and horses and has kept them around her whenever possible. As a child, she was limited to stray dogs, neighbors' horses, and the animals found in library books. But as an adult, she has owned several horses and has worked widely with dogs, both as a veterinarian's assistant and a handler on the dog show circuit.

In recent years Ms. Hall has realized her lifelong dream with the completion of Touchwood, a small, stone hillside cottage planted squarely in the middle of twenty-five acres of woods and hills in northeast Iowa. "I designed the house myself," she writes, "and have had a hand in all phases of its construction, doing all but the heavy work myself, so it is a home in all the best senses of the word."

During the winter, Ms. Hall, the author of several books for young readers, devotes herself to writing. She spends her nonwriting time teaching 4-H dog training classes, competing at dog shows, harvesting mushrooms, ginseng, and firewood, organic gardening, or "just sitting among the unfinished projects and enjoying the breeze, the silence, and the view of the valley."